RAINSONG/SNOWSONG

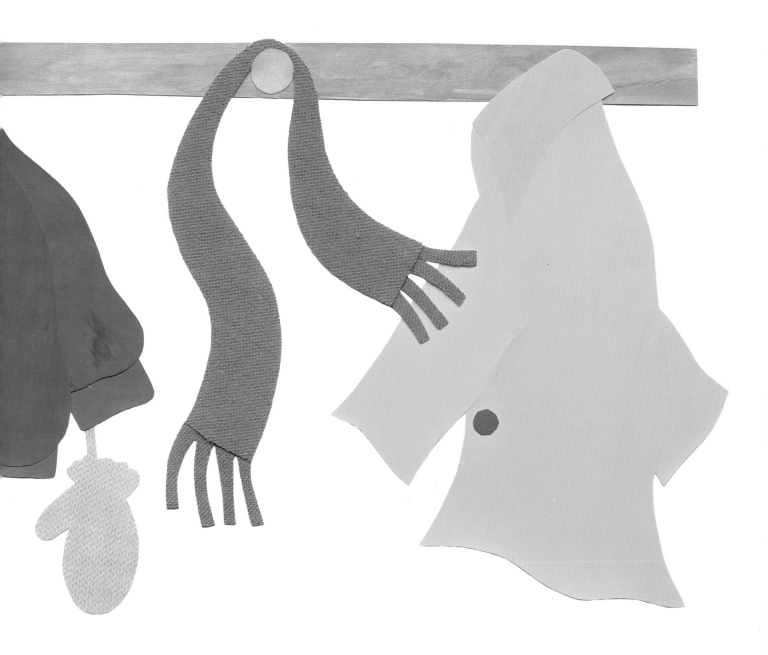

Rainsong

POEMS BY PHILEMON STURGES
PICTURES BY SHARI HALPERN

Snowsong

NORTH-SOUTH BOOKS / NEW YORK / LONDON

Rainsong

The summer rain patters, the summer rain pours,

But I don't need a slicker when *I* am outdoors.

The robin tucks baby bird under her wing,

But I take off my hat when I fly in my swing.

The squirrels stay dry in their nest in the tree,
But *I* like to feel raindrops falling on me.

The butterfly hides so his wings will stay dry,

But I love the shower that falls from the sky.

So when summer rains splatter and summer rains fall,
I like to go splashing in not much at all!

Snowsong

My nose is cold, my cheeks are red,
A flannel scarf's wrapped round my head.

I'm bundled up, 'cause rain, you know,
In wintertime comes down as snow.

Sometimes it sort of spirals round,
Soft fuzzy flakes drift to the ground.

I open wide to catch a few,
But then I notice as I do

That slowly, and without a sound,
Soft snow has pillowed all around.

I make a snowman, angel wings,
And lots of other snowy things.

'Cause when I'm wrapped from head

to toe,

It's fun to frolic in the snow.

To Jesarabit —P.S.
To Kylie, with love —S.H.

Published in the United States by North-South Books Inc., New York.
Published simultaneously in Great Britain, Canada, Australia, and
New Zealand in 1995 by North-South Books, an imprint of
Nord-Süd Verlag AG, Gossau Zürich, Switzerland.

Library of Congress Cataloging-in-Publication Data
Sturges, Philemon.
Rainsong/Snowsong/ by Philemon Sturges; illustrated by Shari Halpern
Summary: Illustrations and rhyming text describe the
joys of playing in the rain and snow.
[1. Rain and rainfall—fiction. 2. Snow—fiction. 3. Stories in rhyme.]
I. Halpern, Shari, Ill. II. Title
PZ8.3.S9227Rai 1995
[E]—dc20 95-954

A CIP catalogue record for this book is available
from The British Library.

The artwork consists of collages made with several different
types of paper painted with acrylics and watercolors, pieces of fabric,
and color photocopies of pieces of fabric.
Typography by Marc Cheshire

ISBN 1-55858-471-4 (trade binding)
1 3 5 7 9 TB 10 8 6 4 2
ISBN 1-55858-472-2 (library binding)
1 3 5 7 9 LB 10 8 6 4 2
Printed in Belgium